There's a UNICORN IN YOUR BOOK

Written by TOM FLETCHER

Illustrated by GREG ABBOTT

Random House New York

For Buzz, Buddy, and Max –T.F.

For Anikka –G.A.

Copyright © 2021 by Tom Fletcher
Illustrated by Greg Abbott

All rights reserved. Published in the United States by Random House Children's Books,
a division of Penguin Random House LLC, New York. Originally published by Puffin Books,
an imprint of Penguin Random House Children's Books U.K., a division of Penguin Random
House U.K., London, in 2021.

Random House and the colophon are registered trademarks of Penguin Random House LLC.

Visit us on the Web! rhcbooks.com

Educators and librarians, for a variety of teaching tools, visit us at RHTeachersLibrarians.com

Library of Congress Cataloging-in-Publication Data is available upon request.
ISBN 978-0-593-43476-5 (trade) — ISBN 978-0-593-43477-2 (ebook)

MANUFACTURED IN CHINA
10 9 8 7 6 5 4 3 2 1
First American Edition

GALLOPING GLITTER!
There's a **UNICORN** in your book!

I bet the next page will be full of
songs about rainbows and sparkles.
Unicorns love to **SING**. . . .

Hmmm . . . this unicorn isn't singing.
What's wrong, Unicorn?

Is there something on the next page
that's making you sad?

Shall we have a look and see?

UH-OH! It's a worry gremlin!

No wonder Unicorn isn't singing—
you don't want a worry gremlin in your book.

Wiggle your fingers to make some
magic dust—that should help.

WOW!

Now there's magic dust everywhere.
(And even

a few

fairies!)

Did it work?
Has the
worry gremlin gone?

SWISH your book
to **SWOOSH** the
dust away.

The worry gremlin is gone! But . . .
Unicorn still isn't singing.
What can we do to cheer him up?

Unicorns love to be tickled under their chins. . . .
Let's try some **TICKLING!**

Oh dear. This unicorn does NOT like tickling.
We should have asked first.

Sorry, Unicorn!

Let's try to make Unicorn smile—
tell your **FUNNIEST JOKE**.

What do you call a
unicorn with a cold?

Well . . . that didn't work at all.

And wait—what are those holes in your book?

Oh no! **MORE** worry gremlins!
They seem to enjoy making Unicorn worry.

How mean!

Try giving your book a **SHAKE**—

that might get rid of them.

OOOOPS!

Now Unicorn's horn is stuck in the page!

Give your book another
SHAKE—really gently. . . .

Well done—Unicorn's free!

Now it's time to get rid of these
worry gremlins once and for all.

I KNOW!

The best way to get rid of a worry
is to tell someone about it.

And I think there might be someone
on the next page who can help us. . . .

It's Unicorn's friend Monster!
That's perfect!

Unicorn, whisper your worry to Monster,
and you'll definitely feel better!

HURRAY! Unicorn is much happier now.
The worry gremlins have started to fade. . . .

Maybe *you* could try
whispering something now.

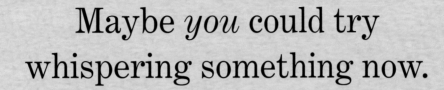

Hold the book very close,
and whisper in Unicorn's ear.

Shhh . . .
whisper really quietly. . . .

Looks like whatever you whispered to Unicorn
made him feel even better—
and now he might be ready to sing!

Shall we join in?

Clear your throat, sit up straight,
and let's count everyone in.

1...2...3...4...

Rainbow sparkle, rainbow sparkle,
shine across the sky!
Makes me happy, makes me happy.
Nobody knows why!

Well done, Unicorn!
Well done, Monster!

And well done, you!

The worry gremlins
          are gone from your book.

          I think it's time to celebrate with . . .

A UNICORN PARTY! Woo-hoo!
Can we give you all a hug?

Then let's give your book a big hug goodbye.